Acel, the Brave Little Star

EMILY BARRETT

To order additional copies of this book, contact:
Xlibris
1-888-795-4274
www.Xlibris.com
Orders@Xlibris.com

Acel, the Brave Little Star

by

EMILY BARRETT

Once upon a time there was a tiny little star named Acel who lived by herself in a very deep, dark hole. Acel was born from a great explosion. Rocks and dust were flung far away, leaving only little Acel behind. The hole was so vast and dark that she could not see anything. But she was very brave and used her own light to illuminate the dark space. Even though she knew she was alone, she never felt lonely.

Acel loved herself completely and found many ways to make herself happy. The little star danced, jumped, skipped and laughed so hard that her light glowed brighter in the big empty space. When her laughter echoed in the dark hole it seemed like there were many other stars, so she was not so alone.

One day the little star was so happy racing across the sky and laughing loudly that she didn't realize she was leaving her deep, dark hole in the sky. Outside it was so bright that she couldn't open her eyes. She called out, "Hello? Is anybody here? I'm Acel, a tiny little star."

When Acel finally opened her eyes, she saw billions of other stars around her. She was so excited, "Wow! So many stars like me!" But, Acel was so small that the other stars didn't see the little star at first. Acel was so curious to learn about this new place that she continued across the sky. The little star traveled for a long time, discovering beautiful spheres of all different colors: orange, green, gray, red, silver, yellow. In a distant corner, Acel glimpsed a beautiful, bright, blue-green sphere. The colors were so radiant that she decided to explore this special sphere.

When she got closer she asked the other stars, "What are these colorful spheres in the sky?" The other stars told Acel, "Those are planets, and that bright blue-green one is Earth. It is a special planet with beautiful gardens with trees and flowers, birds that sing and all kinds of animals. It has everything for humans to play with and have fun."

"What's a human?" Acel asked. "What are they like? Are they like us?" Her star family told the little star, "They are tiny little creatures compared to us. But if you look really hard, you can see them yourself."

The little star was so curious to learn about these tiny beings called humans. So, Acel peered down. She was amazed by their beauty. There was nothing like it in the sky. The flowers, trees, birds and animals were so colorful and fun. "The humans have everything they needed to grow and be happy," thought Acel.

She wanted to know everything about them, so she asked her star family, "Why are they there?" The other stars told Acel, "Humans are part of us. We are both made of the same matter. They are there to experience life." The little star watched the humans for long time. Acel still didn't understand the humans. She didn't understand their actions. So, the little star asked her star-sisters why the humans were unhappy. They told Acel, "The humans are still very young and don't understand their role. They ignore their powers and hurt their planet and all the life on it."

The little star was surprised that beings so radiant didn't see how much they hurt their world. Out of her love for the blue-green planet Acel asked, "How can we help?" Her star family responded, "They are made with the same love we have for one another here in the sky. Long ago we sent our brightest, largest and wisest star-sisters to remind them that all they need to do is to love themselves. But, they have forgotten who they are. There is too much violence now. No star is brave enough to try again."

The little star became very quiet as she thought about the humans. She felt so much love and compassion for the humans and their special planet. Acel decided that she would be brave enough to help the humans. Her star-sisters told little Acel that she would have to become human. But Acel didn't understand.

One of the oldest stars explained to Acel that to become human she must choose her parents. When she finds her parents, she will shoot down out of the sky to become a human baby. "But," the ancient star warned, "you won't remember who you are."

The little tiny star was confused, "How can I help them if I don't remember why am I there?" Her star family reminded Acel, "You help the humans by being the same as you are here: brave and loving. Being yourself is how you help them, setting an example of love, happiness and peace."

And so, brave little Acel began looking for her parents. In a quiet little village on the blue-green planet, Acel spotted a young couple singing to each other as they worked in their colorful garden. Acel loved to dance in the sky, and she imagined dancing to their songs as a small human. The little star knew she had found her parents.

Once Acel found her parents, she felt herself being pulled toward the beautiful planet. Her star-sisters reminded Acel that life as a human would not always be easy, but that she should always love herself. Their voices became very faint until only a whisper. Then everything became silent until she felt herself in a very warm, comfortable and cozy place. She could hear her mother's heartbeat in her womb.

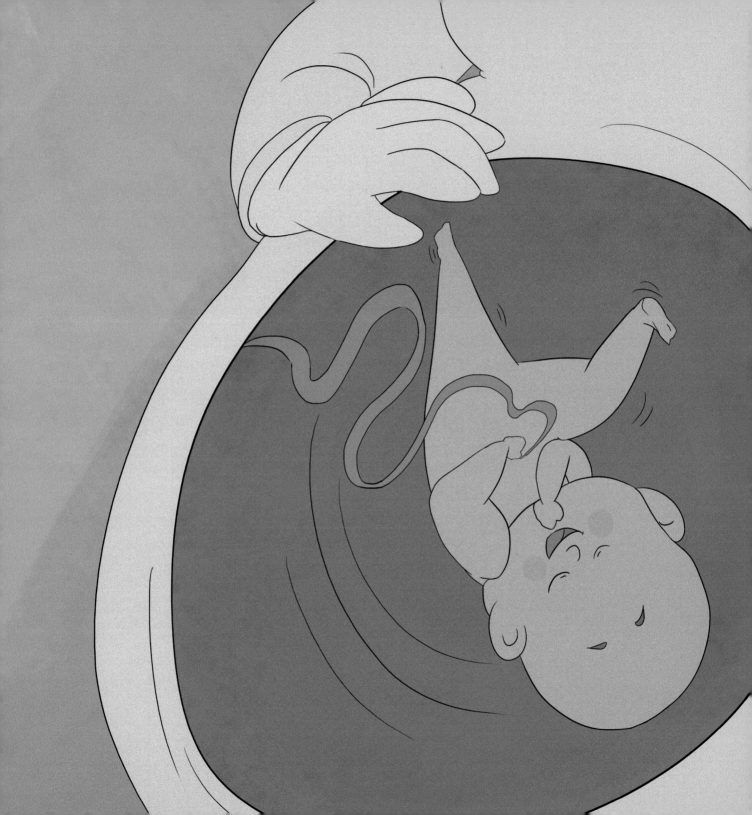

Little by little Acel started to move her fingers, hands and arms. Stretching, kicking and rolling reminded her of dancing and racing across the sky. But soon, Acel began to forget about the sky and her star-sisters.

Finally, it was time for Acel to be born. It was a cold, winter night when Acel met her parents for the first time. As she looked up at her parents' faces, she became completely human. She felt warm arms around her. She opened her big, brown eyes and looked up at her mother, the woman she had chosen, and felt love and peace.

Little Acel had finally brought her love to the blue-green planet. As she grew, Acel would share her gifts with the humans and help them remember who they were even though she had forgotten all about her star-sisters and her sky-home. Her radiant heart was brave enough to love, spreading happiness and peace to all.